Dear Parent:
Your child's love of reading starts here!

Every child learns to read in a different way and at his or her own speed. Some go back and forth between reading levels and read favorite books again and again. Others read through each level in order. You can help your young reader improve and become more confident by encouraging his or her own interests and abilities. From books your child reads with you to the first books he or she reads alone, there are I Can Read Books for every stage of reading:

SHARED READING
Basic language, word repetition, and whimsical illustrations, ideal for sharing with your emergent reader

BEGINNING READING
Short sentences, familiar words, and simple concepts for children eager to read on their own

READING WITH HELP
Engaging stories, longer sentences, and language play for developing readers

READING ALONE
Complex plots, challenging vocabulary, and high-interest topics for the independent reader

I Can Read Books have introduced children to the joy of reading since 1957. Featuring award-winning authors and illustrators and a fabulous cast of beloved characters, I Can Read Books set the standard for beginning readers.

A lifetime of discovery begins with the magical words "I Can Read!"

Visit www.icanread.com for information on enriching your child's reading experience.

For my Metalpig pals

Balzer + Bray is an imprint of HarperCollins Publishers.
I Can Read® and I Can Read Book® are trademarks of HarperCollins Publishers.

Fox versus Winter
Copyright © 2020 by Corey R. Tabor
All rights reserved. Printed in the United States of America.
No part of this book may be used or reproduced in any manner whatsoever without written permission except
in the case of brief quotations embodied in critical articles and reviews. For information address HarperCollins
Children's Books, a division of HarperCollins Publishers, 195 Broadway, New York, NY 10007.
www.icanread.com

Library of Congress Control Number: 2020931656
ISBN 978-0-06-297705-2 (trade bdg.) — ISBN 978-0-06-297704-5 (pbk.)

The artist used pencil, colored pencil, watercolor, and crayon, assembled digitally,
to create the illustrations for this book.
Typography by Honee Jang
Title hand lettering by Alexandra Snowdon
20 21 22 23 24 LSCC 10 9 8 7 6 5 4 3 2 1
❖
First Edition

FOX

versus

WINTER

By **Corey R. Tabor**

BALZER + BRAY

An Imprint of HarperCollinsPublishers

Fox does not like winter.

In winter, Elephant
and the Birds go south.

"Goodbye, Fox!"

says Elephant.

"See you in spring!"
say the Birds.

Bear, Frog, and Turtle
go to bed.

"Good night, Fox!" says Bear.

"See you in spring!" says Frog.

"Glug, glug, glug!" says Turtle.

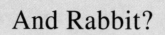

And Rabbit?

Who knows where Rabbit goes?

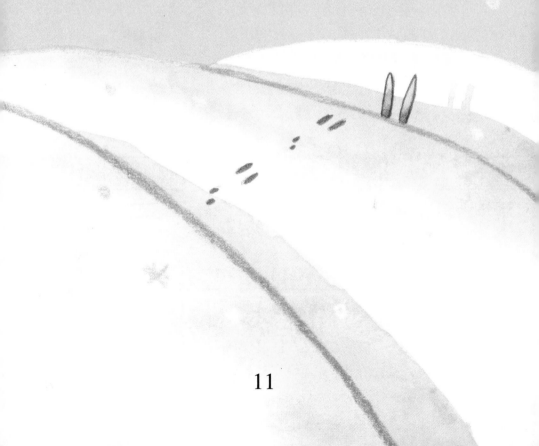

Fox is alone.

Fox is lonely.

"I know," says Fox.

"I will make new friends!"

Fox makes new friends.

"Snowball fight!"

His new friends are not
as good as his old friends.

"I know," says Fox.

"I will go south!"

But Fox is too late.

"I know," says Fox.

"I will go to bed!"

But Fox is too bored.

"I have had it!" yells Fox.

"I will just have to fight winter!"

Fox fights winter.

But winter fights back.

poof

"Oh, boo," says Fox.

"Fox, is that you?"

"It is me," says Fox.

"Rabbit, is that you?"

"It is me," says Rabbit.

"What are you doing?" asks Fox.

"Shh," says Rabbit. "Listen."

Fox listens.

He hears nothing.

Then he hears snow falling.

tap
tap

plop

Fox hears mice moving
under the snow.

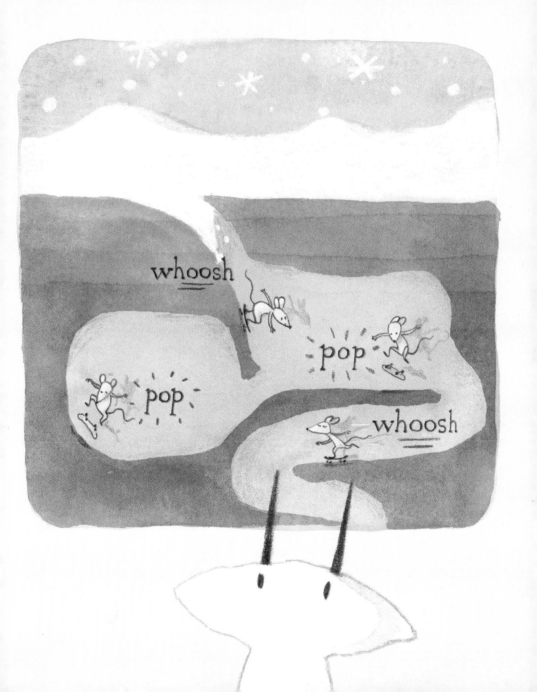

"In winter, I like to be alone,"
says Rabbit.

"I like to sit still and listen."

"Can we be alone together?"
asks Fox.

Rabbit nods.

Fox smiles.

Maybe winter is not so bad.